Scholastic
Clifford THE BIG RED DOG®

Clifford Loves Me!

By Thea Feldman
Illustrated by Gita Lloyd
and Eric Binder

Based on the Scholastic book series
"Clifford The Big Red Dog" by Norman Bridwell.

SCHOLASTIC INC.

New York Toronto London Auckland Sydney
Mexico City New Delhi Hong Kong Buenos Aires

Designed by Peter Koblish

ISBN 0-439-45481-6

10 9 8 7 6 5 4 3 2 03 04 05 06 07

Printed in the U.S.A.
First printing, January 2003

Hi, I'm Emily Elizabeth and
this is Clifford, my Big Red Dog.
Clifford loves living
on Birdwell Island.

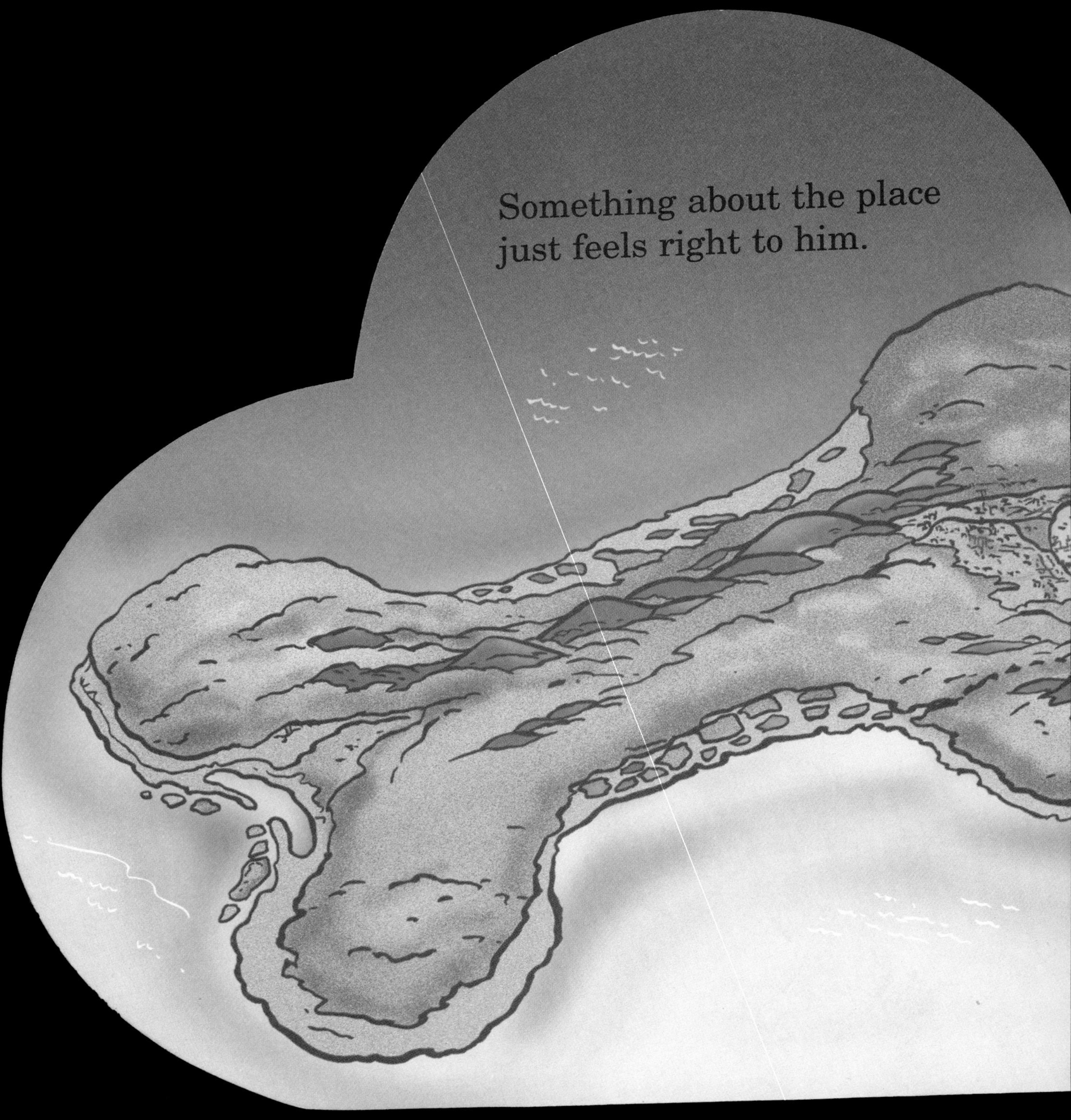

Something about the place
just feels right to him.

While there's one thing Clifford loves best on Birdwell Island, there are many other things he loves, too.

Clifford loves his good friends Cleo and T-Bone. They all love to play and explore the island together.

They also love to dig in
the sand on the beach.

Clifford is very happy when he can uncover buried treasure.

Clifford loves to take a dip in the ocean.

And he loves making a new friend.
But none of that is what Clifford loves best.

Clifford, Cleo, and T-Bone
love to play in the park.
They love to slide . . .

. . . and they love to play
on the seesaw.

Clifford loves to run
into Mr. Bleakman
in the park.

He knows Mr. Bleakman is always
happy to see him. But none of that is
what Clifford loves best, either.

Clifford loves to be helpful, too. He helps Mr. Bleakman with his bird-watching.

Then Clifford helps
rescue a kitten
stuck in a tree.

Clifford also loves
to help Mr. Carlson
deliver the mail.

He helps show visitors around the island, too.

Clifford loves to make his neighbors on Birdwell Island happy by helping out. But that's not what he loves best on Birdwell Island, either.

Clifford loves a good, long dog nap after all his hard work.

STOP

Clifford wakes up to his favorite sound. It's the school bell, signaling the end of the school day. Then Clifford heads as fast as he can toward the school and . . .

. . . Me! Clifford loves me best of all.
And I love Clifford!